Golden Apples

poems for children
chosen by Fiona Waters

Illustrated by Alan Marks

For Judith Elliott
with love and admiration

First published 1985 by William Heinemann Ltd
Piper edition published 1988 by Pan Books Ltd
This edition reprinted 1995 by Macmillan Children's Books
a division of Macmillan Publishers Ltd
25 Eccleston Place, London SW1W 9NF
Basingstoke and Oxford
Associated companies throughout the world

19 18 17

© Fiona Waters 1985

ISBN 0 330 29728 7

Printed and bound in Great Britain by
Mackays of Chatham PLC, Chatham, Kent

Contents

The Song of Wandering
Aengus   W. B. Yeats   11
Hunter Trials   John Betjeman   12
The Frozen Man   Kit Wright   14
Small, Smaller   Russell Hoban   15
The Shell   James Stephens   16
Aunt Julia   Norman MacCaig   18
An Irish Airman Foresees His
Death   W. B. Yeats   20
The Park   James S. Tippett   21
Disturbed, The Cat   Karai Senryū   21
The Starling   John Heath-Stubbs   22
The Late Express   Barbara Giles   23
Junk   Vernon Scannell   24
Fourteen Ways of Touching
the Peter   George MacBeth   26
The Explosion   Philip Larkin   28
In a Station of the Metro   Ezra Pound   29
Until I saw the sea   Lilian Moore   29
Real Life   Gareth Owen   30
Mice   Rose Fyleman   31
Four Seasons   Anon   31
Beachcomber   George Mackay Brown   32
Fireworks   James Reeves   33
Give up Slimming, Mum   Kit Wright   34
A Small Dragon   Brian Patten   36

Fairy Story	Stevie Smith	37
Advertisement	Anon	37
Cycling Down the Street To Meet My Friend John	Gareth Owen	38
Wanted – A Witch's Cat	Shelagh McGee	39
Banananananananana	William Cole	40
A Peculiar Christmas	Roy Fuller	41
Windy Nights	Robert Louis Stevenson	42
To Beat Bad Temper	Cynthia Mitchell	43
Moonlit Apples	John Drinkwater	44
Stopping by Woods on a Snowy Evening	Robert Frost	45
A Child's Calendar	George Mackay Brown	46
Upon a Snail	John Bunyan	47
Flats	Tony Bradman	48
What Has Happened to Lulu?	Charles Causley	49
The Encounter	Clifford Dyment	50
The Night Will Never Stay	Eleanor Farjeon	51
On Tomato Ketchup	Anon	51
Milk for the Cat	Harold Munro	52
The Lion	Jack Prelutsky	53
My Gramp	Derek Stuart	54
Intelligence Test	Vernon Scannell	55
Hugger Mugger	Kit Wright	56
The Rabbit	Alan Brownjohn	58
Stop All the Clocks, Cut Off the Telephone	W. H. Auden	61
The Way Through the Woods	Rudyard Kipling	62
The Scarecrow	Walter de la Mare	64
Winter Days	Gareth Owen	65

Diamond Cut Diamond	Ewart Milne	66
Moon Bat	Sebastian Mays	67
Old English Sheepdog	George MacBeth	68
My Parents	Stephen Spender	69
I Remember, I Remember	Thomas Hood	70
Mare	Judith Thurman	71
Dragon Smoke	Lilian Moore	72
School's Out	William Henry Davies	73
An Old Woman of the Roads	Padraic Colum	74
a cat, a horse and the sun	Roger McGough	75
Bedtime	Allan Ahlberg	76
Lion	Leonard Clark	77
The Muddy Puddle	Dennis Lee	78
The Sandpiper	Robert Frost	79
Timothy Winters	Charles Causley	80
To a Squirrel at Kyle-na-no	W. B. Yeats	81
Babies Are Boring	Peter Mortimer	82
The Listeners	Walter de la Mare	84
The Ptarmigan	Anon	86
Birds' Nests	Edward Thomas	87
Bigtrousers Dan	Peter Mortimer	88
A Visit From St. Nicholas	Clement Clarke Moore	90
Polar Bear	Gail Kredenser	92
Peas	Anon	92
The Tide Rises, The Tide Falls	Henry Wadsworth Longfellow	93
The Discovery	J. C. Squire	94
In the Bathroom	Roy Fuller	95
Zebra	Judith Thurman	95
A Smuggler's Song	Rudyard Kipling	96

Recipe for a Hippopotamus Sandwich	Shel Silverstein	98
The Eagle	Alfred, Lord Tennyson	98
The Wild Dog	Stevie Smith	99
The Collier	Vernon Watkins	100
Overheard on a Saltmarsh	Harold Munro	102
The Fallow Deer at the Lonely House	Thomas Hardy	103
Mushrooms	Sylvia Plath	104
Praise of a Collie	Norman MacCaig	106
You Spotted Snakes	William Shakespeare	107
Silver	Walter de la Mare	108
Copyright acknowledgments		109
Index of authors and first lines		113

Golden Apples

The Song of Wandering Aengus

I went out to the hazel wood,
Because a fire was in my head,
And cut and peeled a hazel wand,
And hooked a berry to a thread;
And when white moths were on the wing,
And moth-like stars were flickering out,
I dropped the berry in a stream
And caught a little silver trout.

When I laid it on the floor
I went to blow the fire aflame,
But something rustled on the floor,
And some one called me by my names
It had become a glimmering girl
With apple blossom in her hair
Who called me by my name and ran
And faded through the brightening air.

Though I am old with wandering
Through hollow lands and hilly lands,
I will find out where she has gone,
And kiss her lips and take her hands;
And walk among long dappled grass,
And pluck till time and times are done
The silver apples of the moon,
The golden apples of the sun.

W. B. YEATS

Hunter Trials

It's awf'lly bad luck on Diana,
    Her ponies have swallowed their bits:
She fished down their throats with a spanner
    And frightened them all into fits.

So now she's attempting to borrow.
    Do lend her some bits, Mummy, *do*;
I'll lend her my own for to-morrow,
    But to-day *I*'ll be wanting them too.

Just look at Prunella on Guzzle,
    The wizardest pony on earth;
Why doesn't she slacken his muzzle
    And tighten the breech in his girth?

I say, Mummy, there's Mrs Geyser
    And doesn't she look pretty sick?
I bet it's because Mona Lisa
    Was hit on the hock with a brick.

Miss Blewitt says Monica threw it,
    But Monica says it was Joan,
And Joan's very thick with Miss Blewitt,
    So Monica's sulking alone.

And Margaret failed in her paces,
    Her withers got tied in a noose,
So her coronets caught in the traces
    And now all her fetlocks are loose.

Oh, it's me now. I'm terribly nervous.
　　I wonder if Smudges will shy.
She's practically certain to swerve as
　　Her Pelham is over one eye.

Oh wasn't it naughty of Smudges?
　　Oh, Mummy, I'm sick with disgust.
She threw me in front of the Judges,
　　And my silly old collarbone's bust.

JOHN BETJEMAN

13

The Frozen Man

Out at the edge of town
where black trees

crack their fingers
in the icy wind

and hedges freeze
on their shadows

and the breath of cattle,
still as boulders,

hangs in rags
under the rolling moon,

a man is walking
alone:

on the coal-black road
his cold

feet
ring

and
ring.

Here in a snug house
at the heart of town

the fire is burning
red and yellow and gold:

you can hear the warmth
like a sleeping cat

breathe softly
in every room.

When the frozen man
comes to the door,

let him in,
let him in,
let him in.

KIT WRIGHT

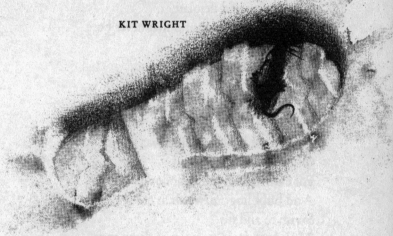

Small, Smaller

I thought that I knew all there was to know
Of being small, until I saw once, black against the snow,
A shrew, trapped in my footprint, jump and fall
And jump again and fall, the hole too deep, the walls too tall.

RUSSELL HOBAN

The Shell

And then I pressed the shell
    Close to my ear
And listened well,
And straightway like a bell
    Came low and clear
The slow, sad murmur of far distant seas,
Whipped by an icy breeze
    Upon a shore
Windswept and desolate,
    It was a sunless strand that never bore
The footprint of a man,
    Nor felt the weight
Since time began
Of any human quality or stir
Save what the dreary winds and waves incur.
And in the hush of waters was the sound
Of pebbles rolling round,
For ever rolling with a hollow sound.
And bubbling sea-weeds as the waters go
Swish to and fro
Their long, cold tentacles of slimy grey.
There was no day,
Nor ever came a night
Setting the stars alight
To wonder at the moon:
Was twilight only and the frightened croon,
Smitten to whimpers, of the dreary wind
And waves that journeyed blind —

And then I loosed my ear – oh, it was sweet
To hear a cart go jolting down the street!

JAMES STEPHENS

Aunt Julia

Aunt Julia spoke Gaelic
very loud and very fast.
I could not answer her –
I could not understand her.

She wore men's boots
when she wore any.
– I can see her strong foot,
stained with peat,
paddling the treadle of the spinningwheel
while her right hand drew yarn
marvellously out of the air.

Hers was the only house
where I've lain at night
in the absolute darkness
of a box bed, listening to
crickets being friendly.

She was buckets
and water flouncing into them.
She was winds pouring wetly
round house-ends.
She was brown eggs, black skirts
and a keeper of threepenny bits
in a teapot.

Aunt Julia spoke Gaelic
very loud and very fast.
By the time I had learned
a little, she lay
silenced in the absolute black
of a sandy grave
at Luskentyre.
But I hear her still, welcoming me
with a seagull's voice
across a hundred yards
of peatscrapes and lazybeds
and getting angry, getting angry
with so many questions
unanswered.

NORMAN MacCAIG

An Irish Airman Foresees His Death

I know that I shall meet my fate
Somewhere among the clouds above;
Those that I fight I do not hate,
Those that I guard I do not love;
My country is Kiltartan Cross,
My countrymen Kiltartan's poor,
No likely end could bring them loss
Or leave them happier than before.
Nor law, nor duty bade me fight,
Nor public men, nor cheering crowds,
A lonely impulse of delight
Drove to this tumult in the clouds;
I balanced all, brought all to mind,
The years to come seemed waste of breath,
A waste of breath the years behind
In balance with this life, this death.

W. B. YEATS

The Park

I'm glad that I
    Live near a park
For in the winter
    After dark
The park lights shine
    As bright and still
As dandelions
    On a hill.

JAMES S. TIPPETT

Disturbed, the Cat

Disturbed, the cat
Lifts its belly
On to its back.

KARAI SENRYŪ

The Starling

The starling is my darling, although
I don't much approve of its
Habits. Proletarian bird,
Nesting in holes and corners, making a mess,
And sometimes dropping its eggs
Just any old where – on the front lawn, for instance.

It thinks it can sing too. In springtime
They are on every rooftop, or high bough,
Or telegraph pole, blithering away
Discords, with clichés picked up
From the other melodists.

But go to Trafalgar Square,
And stand, about sundown, on the steps of St. Martin's;
Mark then, in the air,
The starlings, before they roost, at their evolutions –
Scores of starlings, wheeling,
Streaming and twisting, the whole murmuration
Turning like one bird: an image
Realised, of the City.

JOHN HEATH-STUBBS

The Late Express

There's a train that runs through Hawthorn
3 a.m. or thereabout.
You can hear it hooting sadly,
but no passengers get out.

'That's much too early for a train,'
the station-master said,
'but it's driven by Will Watson
and Willie Watson's dead.'

Poor Willie was a driver
whose record was just fine,
excepting that poor Willie
never learnt to tell the time.

Fathers came home late for dinner,
schoolboys late for their exams,
millionaires had missed on millions,
people changing to the trams.

Oh such fussing and complaining,
even Railways have their pride –
so they sacked poor Willie Watson
and he pined away and died.

Now his ghost reports for duty,
and unrepentant of his crime,
drives a ghost train through here nightly
and it runs to Willie's time.

BARBARA GILES

Junk

It was a leisure-day, called 'holiday'
Only by the very few and old
Though none of these could quite remember why
The word had once possessed a gleam of gold
And still awakened distant silver sounds.
The city glittered; citizens patrolled
The areas reserved for exercise.
Among those walking in the public grounds
A young man and his son, a child of eight,
Moved towards that section of the town
Preserved by civic law in just that state
It wore in 1985, a place
For tourists, amateurs of history
And relic-hunters. There, the man and boy
Stood before a window which displayed
Disordered curiosa: garments, toys,
Primitive machines, containers made
From substances of unknown origin,
Crude metal weapons that, in ancient wars,
Were operated manually. A skin
Of extinct animal, that once was worn
For warmth, and also as a mark of caste,

By someone's female forbear, now adorned
A cabinet composed of genuine wood.
But of that dusty salvage from the past
One object seized the boy's attention: shaped
Like an oblong box, its lifted lid
Showed no interior but solid stuff
In slender layers. Its contents were itself.
The puzzled child said to his father, 'Look!
What's that thing over there?'
                                    The father's brow
Showed momentary perplexity, then cleared:
'Oh that. I think it's what they called a book.'
'What did they use if for?' the child inquired.
'I'm not quite sure. I think my grandpa told me
Long ago, but I've forgotten now.'

VERNON SCANNELL

Fourteen Ways of Touching the Peter

I

You can push
your thumb
in the
ridge
between his
shoulder-blades
to please him.

IV

When he makes
bread,
you can lift
him
by his under-
sides on your
knuckles.

II

Starting
at its root,
you can let
his whole
tail
flow
through your hand.

V

In hot
weather
you can itch
the fur
under
his chin. He
likes that.

VII

Pressing
his head against
your cheek,
you can carry
him
in the dark,
safely.

III

Forming
a fist
you can let
him rub
his bone
skull
against it, hard.

VI

At night
you can hoist
him
out of his bean-stalk,
sleepily
clutching
paper bags.

VIII

In late Autumn
you can find
seeds
adhering
to his fur.
There are
plenty.

IX

You can prise
his jaws
open,
helping
any medicine
he won't
abide, go down.

X

You can touch
his
feet, only
if
he is relaxed.
He
doesn't like it.

XI

You can comb
spare thin
fur
from his coat,
so he won't
get
fur ball.

XII

You can shake
his rigid
chicken‑leg leg,
scouring his
hind‑quarters
with his Vim
tongue.

XIII

Dumping
hot fish
on his plate, you can
fend
him off,
pushing
and purring.

XIV

You can have
him shrimp
along you,
breathing,
whenever
you want
to compose poems.

GEORGE MacBETH

27

The Explosion

On the day of the explosion
Shadows pointed towards the pithead:
In the sun the slagheap slept.

Down the lane came men in pitboots
Coughing oath-edged talk and pipe-smoke,
Shouldering off the freshened silence.

One chased after rabbits; lost them;
Came back with a nest of lark's eggs;
Showed them; lodged them in the grasses.

So they passed in beards and moleskins,
Fathers, brothers, nicknames, laughter,
Through the tall gates standing open.

At noon, there came a tremor; cows
Stopped chewing for a second; sun,
Scarfed as in a heat-haze, dimmed.

The dead go on before us, they
Are sitting in God's house in comfort,
We shall see them face to face —

Plain as lettering in the chapels
It was said, and for a second
Wives saw men of the explosion

Larger than in life they managed —
Gold as on a coin, or walking
Somehow from the sun towards them,

One showing the eggs unbroken.

PHILIP LARKIN

In a Station of the Metro

The apparition of these faces in the crowd;
Petals on a wet, black bough.

EZRA POUND

Until I saw the sea

Until I saw the sea
I did not know
that wind
could wrinkle water so.

I never knew
that sun
could splinter a whole sea of blue.

Nor
did I know before,
a sea breathes in and out
upon a shore.

LILIAN MOORE

Real Life

'Yes,' thought John
his eyes gleaming with excitement
as he looked round the ancient Inn
on the edge of the moors
that was connected to
otherwise inaccessible St Peter's Cove
which had once been a haunt of smugglers
by a secret underground passage
from his bedroom
and which his strange Aunt Lucy
had rented to his mother and father
and Uncle David for
the whole summer holidays,
'Yes this looks just the sort
of place for an adventure but
that kind of thing
only happens in books.'
And he was right.

GARETH OWEN

Mice

I think mice
Are rather nice.

> Their tails are long,
> Their faces small,
> They haven't any
> Chins at all.
> Their ears are pink,
> Their teeth are white,
> They run about
> The house at night.
> They nibble things
> They shouldn't touch
> And no one seems
> To like them much.

But *I* think mice
Are nice.

ROSE FYLEMAN

Four Seasons

Spring is showery, flowery, bowery.
Summer: hoppy, choppy, poppy.
Autumn: wheezy, sneezy, freezy.
Winter: slippy, drippy, nippy.

ANON

Beachcomber

Monday I found a boot —
Rust and salt leather.
I gave it back to the sea, to dance in.

Tuesday a spar of timber worth thirty bob.
Next winter
It will be a chair, a coffin, a bed.

Wednesday a half can of Swedish spirits.
I tilted my head.
The shore was cold with mermaids and angels.

Thursday I got nothing, seaweed,
A whale bone,
Wet feet and a loud cough.

Friday I held a seaman's skull,
Sand spilling from it
The way time is told on kirkyard stones.

Saturday a barrel of sodden oranges.
A Spanish ship
Was wrecked last month at The Kame.

Sunday, for fear of the elders,
I sit on my bum.
What's heaven? A sea chest with a thousand gold coins.

GEORGE MACKAY BROWN

Fireworks

They rise like sudden fiery flowers
    That burst upon the night,
Then fall to earth in burning showers
    Of crimson, blue, and white.

Like buds too wonderful to name,
    Each miracle unfolds,
And catherine-wheels begin to flame
    Like whirling marigolds.

Rockets and Roman candles make
    An orchard of the sky,
Whence magic trees their petals shake
    Upon each gazing eye.

JAMES REEVES

Give up Slimming, Mum

My Mum
is short
and plump
and pretty
and I wish
she'd give up
slimming.

So does Dad.

Her cooking's
delicious —
you can't
beat it —
but you really can
hardly bear
to eat it —
the way she sits
with her eyes
brimming,
watching you
polish off
the spuds
and trimmings
while she
has nothing
herself but a small
thin dry
diet biscuit:
that's all.

My Mum
is short
and plump
and pretty
and I wish
she'd give up
slimming.

So does Dad.

She says she
looks as though
someone had
sat on her —
BUT WE LIKE MUM
WITH A BIT
OF FAT ON HER!

KIT WRIGHT

A Small Dragon

I've found a small dragon in the woodshed.
Think it must have come from deep inside a forest
because it's damp and green and leaves
are still reflecting in its eyes.

I fed it on many things, tried grass,
the roots of stars, hazel‑nut and dandelion,
but it stared up at me as if to say, I need
foods you can't provide.

It made a nest among the coal,
not unlike a bird's but larger,
it is out of place here
and is quite silent.

If you believed in it I would come
hurrying to your house to let you share my wonder,
but I want instead to see
if you yourself will pass this way.

BRIAN PATTEN

Fairy Story

I went into the wood one day
And there I walked and lost my way

When it was so dark I could not see
A little creature came to me

He said if I would sing a song
The time would not be very long

But first I must let him hold my hand tight
Or else the wood would give me a fright

I sang a song, he let me go
But now I am home again there is nobody I know.

STEVIE SMITH

Advertisement

The codfish lays a million eggs,
The helpful hen lays one.
The codfish makes no fuss of its achievement,
The hen boasts what she's done.
We forget the gentle codfish,
The hen we eulogise;
Which teaches us this lesson that —
It pays to advertise!

ANON

Cycling Down the Street to Meet my Friend John

On my bike and down our street,
Swinging round the bend,
Whizzing past the Library,
Going to meet my friend.

Silver flash of spinning spokes,
Whirr of oily chain,
Bump of tyre on railway line
Just before the train.

The road bends sharp at Pinfold Lane
Like a broken arm,
Brush the branches of the trees
Skirting Batty's Farm.

Tread and gasp and strain and bend
Climbing Gallows' Slope,

Flying down the other side
Like an antelope.

Swanking into Johnnie's street,
Cycling hands on hips,
Past O'Connors corner shop
That always smells of chips.

Bump the door of his back-yard
Where we always play,
Lean my bike and knock the door,
'Can John come out to play?'

Wanted – A Witch's Cat

Wanted – a witch's cat.
Must have vigor and spite,
Be expert at hissing,
And good in a fight,
And have balance and poise
On a broomstick at night.

Wanted – a witch's cat.
Must have hypnotic eyes
To tantalize victims
And mesmerize spies,

And be an adept
At scanning the skies.

Wanted – a witch's cat,
With a sly, cunning smile,
A knowledge of spells
And a good deal of guile,
With a fairly hot temper
And plenty of bile.

Wanted – a witch's cat,
Who's not afraid to fly,
For a cat with strong nerves
The salary's high
Wanted – a witch's cat;
Only the best need apply.

SHELAGH MCGEE

Banananananananana

I thought I'd win the spelling bee
   And get right to the top,
But I started to spell "banana,"
   And I didn't know when to stop.

WILLIAM COLE

A Peculiar Christmas

Snow? Absolutely not.
In fact, the weather's quite hot.
At night you can watch this new
Star without catching the 'flu.

Presents? Well, only three.
But then there happen to be
Only three guests. No bells,
No robins, no fir-trees, no smells

— I mean of roast turkey and such:
There are whiffs in the air (a bit much!)
Of beer from the near public house,
And of dirty old shepherds, and cows.

The family party's rather
Small — baby, mother and father —
Uncles, aunts, cousins dispersed.
Well, this Christmas *is* only the first.

ROY FULLER

Windy Nights

Whenever the moon and stars are set,
  Whenever the wind is high,
All night long in the dark and wet,
  A man goes riding by.
Late in the night when the fires are out,
Why does he gallop and gallop about?

Whenever the trees are crying aloud,
  And ships are tossed at sea,
By, on the highway, low and loud,
  By at the gallop goes he.
By at the gallop he goes, and then
By he comes back at the gallop again.

ROBERT LOUIS STEVENSON

To Beat Bad Temper

An angry tiger in a cage
Will roar and roar and roar with rage,
And gnash his teeth and lash his tail,
For that's how tigers rant and rail.
I keep my temper in a cage,
I hate it when it roars with rage,
I hate its teeth, I hate its tail,
So when it starts to rant and rail,
I tell my mum, I tell my dad,
I tell them why it's feeling bad,
And then I skip and skip and skip,
And lash my rope just like a whip,
And when I skip because I'm cross,
My temper-tiger knows who's boss,
And when I've skipped and whipped like mad,
My temper-tiger's not so bad.
I have to keep it tame this way,
Or it will eat me up one day.

CYNTHIA MITCHELL

Moonlit Apples

At the top of the house the apples are laid in rows,
And the skylight lets the moonlight in, and those
Apples are deep-sea apples of green. There goes
   A cloud on the moon in the autumn night.

A mouse in the wainscot scratches, and scratches, and then
There is no sound at the top of the house of men
Or mice; and the cloud is blown, and the moon again
   Dapples the apples with deep-sea light.

They are lying in rows there, under the gloomy beams;
On the sagging floor; they gather the silver streams
Out of the moon, those moonlit apples of dreams,
   And quiet is the steep stair under.

In the corridors under there is nothing but sleep,
And stiller than ever on orchard boughs they keep
Tryst with the moon, and deep is the silence, deep
   On moon-washed apples of wonder.

JOHN DRINKWATER

Stopping by Woods on a Snowy Evening

Whose woods these are I think I know.
His house is in the village, though;
He will not see me stopping here
To watch his woods fill up with snow.

My little horse must think it queer
To stop without a farmhouse near
Between the woods and frozen lake
The darkest evening of the year.

He gives his harness bells a shake
To ask if there is some mistake.
The only other sound's the sweep
Of easy wind and downy flake.

The woods are lovely, dark, and deep,
But I have promises to keep,
And miles to go before I sleep,
And miles to go before I sleep.

ROBERT FROST

A Child's Calendar

No visitors in January.
A snowman smokes a cold pipe in the yard.

They stand about like ancient women,
The February hills.
They have seen many a coming and going, the hills.

In March Moorfea is littered
With knock-kneed lambs.

Daffodils at the door in April,
Three shawled Marys.
A lark splurges in galilees of sky.

And in May
A russet stallion shoulders the hill apart.
The mares tremble.

The June bee
Bumps in the pane with a heavy bag of plunder.

Strangers swarm in July
With cameras, binoculars, bird books.

He thumped the crag in August,
A blind blue whale.

September crofts get wrecked in blond surges.
They struggle, the harvesters.
They drag loaf and ale-kirn into winter.

In October the fishmonger
Argues, pleads, threatens at the shore.

Nothing in November
But tinkers at the door, keening, with cans.

Some December midnight
Christ, lord, lie warm in our byre.
Here are stars, an ox, poverty enough.

GEORGE MACKAY BROWN

Upon a Snail

She goes but softly, but she goeth sure,
She stumbles not, as stronger creatures do;
Her journey's shorter, so she may endure
Better than they which do much further go.

She makes no noise, but stilly seizeth on
The flower or herb appointed for her food;
The which she quietly doth feed upon,
While others range, and glare, but find no good.

And though she doth but very softly go,
However slow her pace be, yet 'tis sure;
And certainly they that do travel so,
The prize which they do aim at, they procure.

JOHN BUNYAN

Flats

I've always wanted to live in a house
  with stairs
I've always lived in flats
  and that's
what I don't like about them
  they're flat
and you can never get away from
  your mum
or your sister and her boyfriend
  or your
little brother and his mates, they're
  always squeezed
into the front room all together with
  the fire
on, breathing each other's air.
  If I
lived in a house with stairs
  I could
get away up there

TONY BRADMAN

What Has Happened to Lulu?

What has happened to Lulu, mother?
    What has happened to Lu?
There's nothing in her bed but an old rag-doll
    And by its side a shoe.

Why is her window wide, mother,
    The curtain flapping free,
And only a circle on the dusty shelf
    Where her money-box used to be?

Why do you turn your head, mother,
    And why do the tear-drops fall?
And why do you crumple that note on the fire
    And say it is nothing at all?

I woke to voices late last night,
    I heard an engine roar.
Why do you tell me the things I heard
    Were a dream and nothing more?

I heard somebody cry, mother,
    In anger or in pain,
But now I ask you why, mother,
    You say it was a gust of rain.

Why do you wander about as though
    You don't know what to do?
What has happened to Lulu, mother?
    What has happened to Lu?

CHARLES CAUSLEY

The Encounter

Over the grass a hedgehog came
Questing the air for scents of food
And the cracked twig of danger.
He shuffled near in the gloom. Then stopped.
He was sure aware of me. I went up,
Bent low to look at him, and saw
His coat of lances pointing to my hand.
What could I do
To show I was no enemy?
I turned him over, inspected his small clenched paws,
His eyes expressionless as glass,
And did not know how I could speak,
By touch or tongue, the language of a friend.

It was a grief to be a friend
Yet to be dumb; to offer peace
And bring the soldiers out . . .

CLIFFORD DYMENT

The Night Will Never Stay

The night will never stay,
The night will still go by,
Though with a million stars
You pin it to the sky;

Though you bind it with the blowing wind
And buckle it with the moon,
The night will slip away
Like sorrow or a tune.

ELEANOR FARJEON

On Tomato Ketchup

If you do not shake the bottle,
None'll come, and then a lot'll.

ANON

Milk for the Cat

When the tea is brought at five o'clock,
And all the neat curtains are drawn with care,
The little black cat with bright green eyes
Is suddenly purring there.

At first she pretends, having nothing to do,
She has come in merely to blink by the grate,
But, though tea may be late or the milk may be sour,
She is never late.

And presently her agate eyes
Take a soft large milky haze,
And her independent casual glance
Becomes a stiff, hard gaze.

Then she stamps her claws or lifts her ears,
Or twists her tail and begins to stir,
Till suddenly all her lithe body becomes
One breathing, trembling purr.

The children eat and wriggle and laugh;
The two old ladies stroke their silk:
But the cat is grown small and thin with desire,
Transformed to a creeping lust for milk.

The white saucer like some full moon descends
At last from the clouds of the table above;
She sighs and dreams and thrills and glows,
Transfigured with love.

She nestles over the shining rim,
Buries her chin in the creamy sea;
Her tail hangs loose; each drowsy paw
Is doubled under each bending knee.

A long, dim ecstasy holds her life;
Her world is an infinite shapeless white,
Till her tongue has curled the last holy drop,
Then she sinks back into the night,

Draws and dips her body to heap
Her sleepy nerves in the great arm-chair,
Lies defeated and buried deep
Three or four hours unconscious there.

HAROLD MONRO

The Lion

The lion has a golden mane
and under it a clever brain.
He lies around and idly roars
and lets the lioness do the chores.

JACK PRELUTSKY

My Gramp

My gramp has got a medal.
On the front there is a runner.
On the back it says:
Senior Boys 100 Yards
First William Green
I asked him about it,
but before he could reply
Gran said, 'Don't listen to his tales.
The only running he ever did
was after the girls.'
Gramp gave a chuckle
and went out the back
to get the tea.
As he shuffled down the passage
with his back bent,
I tried to imagine him,
legs flying, chest out,
breasting the tape.
But I couldn't.

DEREK STUART

Intelligence Test

'What do you use your eyes for?'
The white-coated man enquired.
'I use my eyes for looking,'
Said Toby, ' – unless I'm tired.'

'I see. And then you close them,'
Observed the white-coated man.
'Well done. A very good answer.
Let's try another one.'

'What is your nose designed for?
And what use is the thing to you?'
'I use my nose for smelling,'
Said Toby. 'Don't you, too?'

'I do indeed,' said the expert,
'That's what the thing is for.
Now I've another question to ask you,
Then there won't be any more.'

'What are your ears intended for?
Those things at each side of your head?
Come on – don't be shy – I'm sure you can say.'
'For washing behind,' Toby said.

VERNON SCANNELL

Hugger Mugger

I'd sooner be
Jumped and thumped and dumped

I'd sooner be
Slugged and mugged . . . than *hugged* . . .

And clobbered with a slobbering
Kiss by Auntie Jean:

You know what I mean:

Whenever she comes to stay,
You know you're bound

To get one.
A quick
   short
   peck
   would
   be
   O.K.
But this is a
Whacking great
Smacking great
Wet one!

All whoosh and spit
And crunch and squeeze
And '*Dear* little boy!'
And 'Auntie's missed you!'

And 'Come to Auntie, she
Hasn't *kissed* you!'
Please don't do it, Auntie,
PLEASE!

Or if you've absolutely
Got to,

And nothing on *earth* can persuade you
Not to,

The trick
Is to make it
Quick,

You know what I mean?

For as things are,
I really would far,

Far sooner be
Jumped and thumped and dumped,

I'd sooner be
Slugged and mugged . . . than *hugged* . . .

And clobbered with a slobbering
Kiss by my Auntie

Jean!

KIT WRIGHT

The Rabbit

We are going to see the rabbit.
We are going to see the rabbit.
Which rabbit, people say?
Which rabbit, ask the children?
Which rabbit?
The only rabbit,
The only rabbit in England,
Sitting behind a barbed-wire fence
Under the floodlights, neon lights,
Sodium lights,
Nibbling grass
On the only patch of grass
In England, in England
(Except the grass by the hoardings
Which doesn't count.)
We are going to see the rabbit
And we must be there on time.

First we shall go by escalator,
Then we shall go by underground,
And then we shall go by motorway
And then by helicopterway,
And the last ten yards we shall have to go
On foot.

And now we are going
All the way to see the rabbit,
We are nearly there,
We are longing to see it,

And so is the crowd
Which is here in thousands
With mounted policemen
And big loudspeakers
And bands and banners,
And everyone has come a long way.
But soon we shall see it
Sitting and nibbling
The blades of grass
On the only patch of grass
In — but something has gone wrong!

Why is everyone so angry,
Why is everyone jostling
And slanging and complaining?

The rabbit has gone,
Yes, the rabbit has gone.
He has actually burrowed down into the earth
And made himself a warren, under the earth,
Despite all these people.
And what shall we do?
What *can* we do?

It is all a pity, you must be disappointed,
Go home and do something else for today,
Go home again, go home for today.
For you cannot hear the rabbit, under the earth,
Remarking rather sadly to himself, by himself,
As he rests in his warren, under the earth:
'It won't be long, they are bound to come,
They are bound to come and find me, even here.'

ALAN BROWNJOHN

Stop All the Clocks, Cut Off the Telephone

Stop all the clocks, cut off the telephone,
Prevent the dog from barking with a juicy bone,
Silence the pianos and with muffled drum
Bring out the coffin, let the mourners come.

Let aeroplanes circle moaning overhead
Scribbling on the sky the message He Is Dead,
Put the crêpe bows round the white necks of the public doves,
Let the traffic policemen wear black cotton gloves.

He was my North, my South, my East and West,
My working week and my Sunday rest,
My noon, my midnight, my talk, my song;
I thought that love would last for ever: I was wrong.

The stars are not wanted now: put out every one;
Pack up the moon and dismantle the sun;
Pour away the ocean and sweep up the wood.
For nothing now can ever come to any good.

W. H. AUDEN

The Way Through the Woods

They shut the road through the woods
Seventy years ago.
Weather and rain have undone it again,
And now you would never know
There was once a road through the woods
Before they planted the trees.
It is underneath the coppice and heath
And the thin anemones.
Only the keeper sees
That, where the ring-dove broods,
And the badgers roll at ease,
There was once a road through the woods.

Yet, if you enter the woods
Of a summer evening late,
When the night-air cools on the trout-ringed pools
Where the otter whistles his mate,
(They fear not men in the woods,
Because they see so few.)
You will hear the beat of a horse's feet,
And the swish of a skirt in the dew,
Steadily cantering through
The misty solitudes,
As though they perfectly knew
The old lost road through the woods . . .
But there is no road through the woods.

RUDYARD KIPLING

The Scarecrow

All winter through I bow my head
   Beneath the driving rain;
The North Wind powders me with snow
   And blows me black again;
At midnight in a maze of stars
   I flame with glittering rime,
And stand, above the stubble, stiff
   As mail at morning-prime.
But when that child, called Spring, and all
   His host of children, come,
Scattering their buds and dew upon
   These acres of my home,
Some rapture in my rags awakes;
   I lift void eyes and scan
The skies for crows, those ravening foes,
   Of my strange master, Man.
I watch him striding lank behind
   His clashing team, and know
Soon will the wheat swish body high
   Where once lay sterile snow;
Soon I shall gaze across the sea
   Of sun-begotten grain,
Which my unflinching watch hath sealed
   For harvest once again.

WALTER DE LA MARE

Winter Days

Biting air
Winds blow
City streets
Under snow

_____y eyes
Hands raw

Chimneys smoke
Cars crawl
Piled snow
On garden wall

Slush in gutters
Ice in lanes
Frosty patterns
On window panes

Morning call
Lift up head
Nipped by winter
Stay in bed

GARETH OWEN

Diamond Cut Diamond

Two cats
One up a tree
One under the tree
The cat up the tree is he
The cat under the tree is she
The tree is witch elm, just incidentally,
He takes no notice of she, she takes no notice of he.
He stares at the woolly clouds passing, she stares at the tree.
There's been a lot written about cats, by Old Possum, Yeats and Company
But not Alfred de Musset or Lord Tennyson or Poe or anybody
Wrote about one cat under, and one cat up, a tree.
God knows why this should be left to me
Except I like cats as cats be
Especially one cat up
And one cat under
A witch elm
Tree.

EWART MILNE

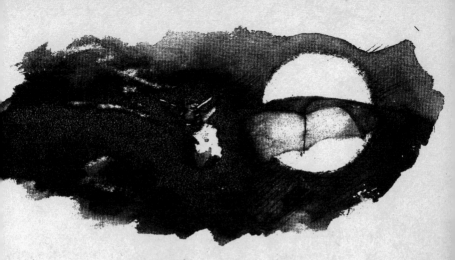

Moon Bat

Once I held a bat, its small helpless
body quivering in my hand.
Its silver grey body like moonlight
shining on ancient web.
Its small shiny eyes had a look
of fear as it stared intently at
me.
I was filled with delight as moonlight shone through the veil-like
membrane of its wings.
As I lifted my hand to the starry
night, its frail wings lifted it up to
the moon.

SEBASTIAN MAYS (Age 10)

Old English Sheep-dog

Eyes
drowned in fur:
an affectionate,

rough, cumulus
cloud, licking
wrists and

panting, fur
too hot
in your

'profuse' coat
of old wool. You
bundle yourself

about on
four shaggy
pillars

of Northumberland
lime/stone,
gathering sheep.

GEORGE MacBETH

My Parents

My parents kept me from the children who were rough.
Who threw words like stones and who wore torn clothes.
Their thighs showed through rags. They ran in the street
And climbed cliffs and stripped by the country streams.

I feared more than tigers their muscles like iron
Their jerking hands and their knees tight on my arms.
I feared the salt coarse pointing of those boys
Who copied my lisp behind me on the road.

They were lithe, they sprang out behind hedges
Like dogs to bark at my world. They threw mud
While I looked the other way, pretending to smile.
I longed to forgive them, but they never smiled.

STEPHEN SPENDER

I Remember, I Remember

I remember, I remember,
The house where I was born,
The little window where the sun
Came peeping in at morn;
He never came a wink too soon,
Nor brought too long a day,
But now, I often wish the night
Had borne my breath away!

I remember, I remember,
The roses, red and white,
The violets, and the lily-cups,
Those flowers made of light!
The lilacs where the robin built,
And where my brother set
The laburnum on his birth-day, –
The tree is living yet!

I remember, I remember,
Where I was used to swing.
And thought the air must rush as fresh
To swallows on the wing;
My spirit flew in feathers then,
That is so heavy now,
And summer pools could hardly cool
The fever on my brow!

I remember, I remember,
The fir trees dark and high;

I used to think their slender tops
Were close against the sky;
It was a childish ignorance,
But now 'tis little joy
To know I'm farther off from heaven
Than when I was a boy.

THOMAS HOOD

Mare

When the mare shows you
her yellow teeth, stuck
with clover and gnawed leaf,
you know they have combed
pastures of spiky grasses,
and tough thickets.

But when you offer her
a sweet, white lump
from the trembling plate
of your palm – she trots
to the gate, sniffs –
and takes it with velvet lips.

JUDITH THURMAN

Dragon Smoke

Breathe and blow
white clouds
   with every puff.
It's cold today,
   cold enough
to see your breath.
Huff!
    Breathe dragon smoke
    today!

LILIAN MOORE

School's Out

Girls scream,
    Boys shout;
Dogs bark,
    School's out.

Cats run,
    Horses shy;
Into trees
    Birds fly.

Babes wake
    Open-eyed;
If they can,
    Tramps hide.

Old man,
    Hobble home;
Merry mites,
    Welcome.

WILLIAM HENRY DAVIES

An Old Woman of the Roads

O, to have a little house!
  To own the hearth and stool and all!
The heaped-up sods upon the fire,
  The pile of turf against the wall!

To have a clock with weights and chains
  And pendulum swinging up and down!
A dresser filled with shining delph,
  Speckled and white and blue and brown!

I could be busy all the day
  Clearing and sweeping hearth and floor,
And fixing on their shelf again
  My white and blue and speckled store!

I could be quiet there at night
  Beside the fire and by myself,
Sure of a bed, and loth to leave
  The ticking clock and shining delph!

Och! but I'm weary of mist and dark,
  And roads where there's never a house or bush,
And tired I am of bog and road
  And the crying wind and lonesome hush!

And I am praying to God on high,
  And I am praying Him night and day,
For a little house — a house of my own —
  Out of the wind's and the rain's way.

PADRAIC COLUM

a cat, a horse and the sun

a cat mistrusts the sun
keeps out of its way
only where sun and shadow meet
it moves

a horse loves the sun
it basks all day
snorts
and beats its hooves

the sun likes horses
but hates cats
that is why it makes hay
and heats tin roofs

ROGER MCGOUGH

Bedtime

When I go upstairs to bed,
I usually give a loud cough.
This is to scare The Monster off.

When I come to my room,
I usually slam the door right back.
This is to squash The Man in Black
Who sometimes hides there.

Nor do I walk to the bed,
But usually run and jump instead.
This is to stop The Hand –
Which is under there all right –
From grabbing my ankles.

ALLAN AHLBERG

Lion

Poor prisoner in a cage,
I understand your rage
Any why you loudly roar
Walking that stony floor.

Your forest eyes are sad
As wearily you pad
A few yards up and down,
A king without a crown.

Up and down all day.
A wild beast for display,
Or lying in the heat
With sawdust, smells and meat,

Remembering how you chased
Your jungle prey, and raced,
Leaping upon their backs
Along the grassy tracks.

But you are here instead,
Better, perhaps, be dead
Than locked in this dark den;
Forgive us, lion, then,
Who did not ever choose,
Our circuses and zoos.

LEONARD CLARK

The Muddy Puddle

I am sitting
In the middle
Of a rather Muddy
Puddle,
With my bottom
Full of bubbles
And my rubbers
Full of Mud,

While my jacket
And my sweater
Go on slowly
Getting wetter
As I very
Slowly settle
To the Bottom
Of the Mud.

And I find that
What a person
With a puddle
Round his middle
Thinks of mostly
In the muddle
Is the Muddi-
Ness of Mud.

DENNIS LEE

The Sandpiper

At the edge of tide
He stops to wonder,
Races through
The lace of thunder.

On toothpick legs
Swift and brittle,
He runs and pipes
And his voice is little.

But small or not,
He has a notion
To outshout
The Atlantic Ocean.

ROBERT FROST

Timothy Winters

Timothy Winters comes to school
With eyes as wide as a football pool,
Ears like bombs and teeth like splinters:
A blitz of a boy is Timothy Winters.

His belly is white, his neck is dark,
And his hair is an exclamation mark.
His clothes are enough to scare a crow
And through his britches the blue winds blow.

When teacher talks he won't hear a word
And shoots down dead the arithmetic-bird,
He licks the patterns off his plate
And he's not even heard of the Welfare State.

Timothy Winters has bloody feet
And he lives in a house on Suez Street,
He sleeps in a sack on the kitchen floor
And they say there aren't boys like him any more.

Old Man Winters likes his beer
And his missus ran off with a bombardier,
Grandma sits in the grate with a gin
And Timothy's dosed with an aspirin.

The Welfare Worker lies awake
But the law's as tricky as a ten-foot snake,
So Timothy Winters drinks his cup
And slowly goes on growing up.

At Morning Prayers the Headmaster helves
For children less fortunate than ourselves,
And the loudest response in the room is when
Timothy Winters roars 'Amen!'

So come one angel, come on ten:
Timothy Winters says 'Amen'
Amen amen amen amen.
Timothy Winters, Lord.
                           Amen.

CHARLES CAUSLEY

To a Squirrel at Kyle-Na-No

Come play with me;
Why should you run
Through the shaking tree
As though I'd a gun
To strike you dead?
When all I would do
Is to scratch your head
And let you go.

W. B. YEATS

Babies are Boring

Babies are boring
(Oh yes they are!)
Don't believe mothers
or a doting papa.
Babies are boring,
their hands and their bellies,

their pink puffy faces
which wobble like jellies.
Accountants and grandmas
and sailors from Chile
when faced with a baby
act extraordinarily silly.
They grimace and they giggle,
say 'diddle-dum-doo',
they waggle their fingers
(stick their tongues out too).
They slaver and slurp
then they tickle its tummy,
they gurgle and drool:
'Oh, he's just like his mummy!'
'Oh, his mouth is like Herbert's!'
'He's got Uncle Fred's nose!'
'My word, he looks healthy!'
'It's his feed, I suppose?'
Save me from baldness
and the old smell of kippers,
but most of all save me
from all gooey nippers.
I'm a brute, I'm a fiend
and no use to implore me
to tickle its chin,
because all babies bore me.

PETER MORTIMER

The Listeners

'Is there anybody there?' said the Traveller,
    Knocking on the moonlit door;
And his horse in the silence champed the grasses
    Of the forest's ferny floor:
And a bird flew up out of the turret,
    Above the Traveller's head:
And he smote upon the door again a second time;
    'Is there anybody there?' he said.
But no one descended to the Traveller;
    No head from the leaf-fringed sill
Leaned over and looked into his grey eyes.
    Where he stood perplexed and still.
But only a host of phantom listeners
    That dwelt in the lone house then
Stood listening in the quiet of the moonlight
    To that voice from the world of men:
Stood thronging the faint moonbeams on the dark stair,
    That goes down to the empty hall,
Hearkening in an air stirred and shaken
    By the lonely Traveller's call.
And he felt in his heart their strangeness,
    Their stillness answering his cry,
While his horse moved, cropping the dark turf,
    'Neath the starred and leafy sky;
For he suddenly smote on the door, even
    Louder, and lifted his head:—

'Tell them I came, and no one answered,
    That I kept my word,' he said.
Never the least stir made the listeners,
    Though every word he spake
Fell echoing through the shadowiness of the still house
    From the one man left awake:
Ay, they heard his foot upon the stirrup,
    And the sound of iron on stone,
And how the silence surged softly backward,
    When the plunging hoofs were gone.

WALTER DE LA MARE

The Ptarmigan

The ptarmigan is strange,
As strange as he can be;
Never sits on ptelephone poles
Or roosts upon a ptree.
And the way he ptakes pto spelling
Is the strangest thing pto me.

ANON

Birds' Nests

The summer nests uncovered by autumn wind,
Some torn, others dislodged, all dark,
Everyone sees them: low or high in tree,
Or hedge, or single bush, they hang like a mark.

Since there's no need of eyes to see them with
I cannot help a little shame
That I missed most, even at eye's level, till
The leaves blew off and made the seeing no game.

'Tis a light pang. I like to see the nests
Still in their places, now first known,
At home and by far roads. Boys never found them,
Whatever jays or squirrels may have done.

And most I like the winter nest deep-hid
That leaves and berries fell into;
Once a dormouse dined there on hazel nuts;
And grass and goose-grass seeds found soil and grew.

EDWARD THOMAS

Bigtrousers Dan

In the land of Rumplydoodle
where men eat jollips for tea,
and the cows in the hay
feel sleepy all day,
there's a wonderful sight to see.
On the banks of the River Bongbong,
in a hut made of turnips and cream,
sits a whiskery man,
name of Bigtrousers Dan,
and he plays with his brand new machine.
There are gronfles
and nogglets
and pluffles
and valves that go
ker-pling and ker-plang,

and a big sugar wheel
that revolves with a squeal
'till it's oiled with a chocolate meringue.
There are wurdlies
and flumdings
and crumchies
that go round just as fast as they can,
and a big choolate ball
that makes no sound at all,
thanks to clever old
Bigtrousers Dan.

PETER MORTIMER

A Visit From St. Nicholas

'Twas the night before Christmas, when all through the house
Not a creature was stirring, not even a mouse;
The stockings were hung by the chimney with care,
In hopes that St. Nicholas soon would be there;
The children were nestled all snug in their beds,
While visions of sugar-plums danced in their heads;
And mamma in her 'kerchief, and I in my cap,
Had just settled our brains for a long winter's nap —
When out on the lawn there arose such a clatter,
I sprang from my bed to see what was the matter.
Away to the window I flew like a flash,
Tore open the shutters, and threw up the sash.
The moon, on the breast of the new-fallen snow,
Gave the lustre of midday to objects below;
When, what to my wondering eyes should appear,
But a miniature sleigh and eight tiny reindeer,
With a little old driver, so lively and quick,
I knew in a moment it must be St. Nick.
More rapid than eagles his coursers they came,
And he whistled, and shouted, and called them by name:
'Now, *Dasher*! now, *Dancer*! now, *Prancer* and *Vixen*!
On, *Comet*! on, *Cupid*! on, *Donder* and *Blitzen*!
To the top of the porch! to the top of the wall!
Now dash away! dash away! dash away all!'
As dry leaves that before the wild hurricane fly,
When they meet with an obstacle, mount to the sky;
So up to the house-top the coursers they flew
With the sleigh full of toys, and St. Nicholas too.

And then, in a twinkling, I heard on the roof
The prancing and pawing of each little hoof –
As I drew in my head, and was turning around,
Down the chimney St. Nicholas came with a bound.
He was dressed all in fur, from his head to his foot,
And his clothes were all tarnished with ashes and soot;
A bundle of toys he had flung on his back,
And he looked like a pedlar just opening his pack.
His eyes – how they twinkled; his dimples, how merry!
His cheeks were like roses, his nose like a cherry!
His droll little mouth was drawn up like a bow,
And the beard of his chin was as white as the snow;
The stump of a pipe he held tight in his teeth,
And the smoke it encircled his head like a wreath;
He had a broad face and a little round belly
That shook, when he laughed, like a bowl full of jelly.
He was chubby and plump, a right jolly old elf,
And I laughed when I saw him, in spite of myself;
A wink of his eye and a twist of his head
Soon gave me to know I had nothing to dread;
He spoke not a word, but went straight to his work,
And filled all the stockings; then turned with a jerk,
And laying his finger aside of his nose,
And giving a nod, up the chimney he rose;
He sprang to his sleigh, to his team gave a whistle,
And away they all flew like the down of a thistle.
But I heard him exclaim, ere he drove out of sight,
'*Happy Christmas to all, and to all a good night!*'

CLEMENT CLARKE MOORE

Polar Bear

The secret of the polar bear
Is that he wears long underwear.

GAIL KREDENSER

Peas

I eat my peas with honey,
I've done it all my life,
They do taste kind of funny,
But it keeps them on the knife.

ANON

The Tide Rises, The Tide Falls

The tide rises, the tide falls,
The twilight darkens, the curlew calls;
Along the sea-sands damp and brown
The traveller hastens towards the town,
    And the tide rises, the tide falls.

Darkness settles on roofs and walls,
But the sea, the sea in the darkness calls;
The little waves, with their soft, white hands,
Efface the footprints in the sands,
    And the tide rises, the tide falls.

The morning breaks; the steeds in their stalls
Stamp and neigh, as the hostler calls;
The day returns, but nevermore
Returns the traveller to the shore,
    And the tide rises, the tide falls.

HENRY WADSWORTH LONGFELLOW

The Discovery

There was an Indian, who had known no change,
Who strayed content along a sunlit beach
Gathering shells. He heard a sudden strange
Commingled noise; looked up; and gasped for speech.
For in the bay, where nothing was before,
Moved on the şea, by magic, huge canoes,
With bellying cloths on poles, and not one oar,
And fluttering coloured signs and clambering crews.

And he, in fear, this naked man alone,
His fallen hands forgetting all their shells,
His lips gone pale, knelt low behind a stone,
And stared, and saw, and did not understand,
Columbus' doom-burdened caravels
Slant to the shore, and all their seamen land.

J. C. SQUIRE

In the Bathroom

What is that blood-stained thing –
Hairy, as if it were frayed –
Stretching itself along
The slippery bath's steep side?

I approach it, ready to kill,
Or run away, aghast;
And find I have to deal
With a used elastoplast.

ROY FULLER

Zebra

white sun
black
fire escape,

morning
grazing like a zebra
outside my window.

JUDITH THURMAN

A Smuggler's Song

If you wake at midnight and hear a horse's feet,
Don't go drawing back the blind, or looking in the street,
Them that asks no questions isn't told a lie.
Watch the wall, my darling, while the Gentlemen go by!
　　　Five and twenty ponies,
　　　Trotting through the dark –
　　　Brandy for the Parson,
　　　Baccy for the Clerk;
　　　Laces for a lady; letters for a spy,
And watch the wall, my darling, while the Gentlemen go by!

Running round the woodlump if you chance to find
Little barrels, roped and tarred, all full of brandy-wine;
Don't you shout to come and look, nor take 'em for your play;
Put the brushwood back again, – and they'll be gone next day!

If you see the stableyard setting open wide;
If you see a tired horse lying down inside;
If your mother mends a coat cut about and tore;
If the lining's wet and warm – don't you ask no more!

If you meet King George's men, dressed in blue and red,
You be careful what you say, and mindful what is said.
If they call you "pretty maid", and chuck you 'neath the chin,
Don't you tell where no one is, nor yet where no one's been!

Knocks and footsteps round the house – whistles after dark –
You've no call for running out till the housedogs bark.
Trusty's here and Pincher's here, and see how dumb they lie –
They don't fret to follow when the Gentlemen go by!

If you do as you've been told, likely there's a chance,
You'll be give a dainty doll, – all the way from France,
With a cap of Valenciennes, and a velvet hood –
A present from the Gentlemen, along o' being good!
       Five and twenty ponies,
       Trotting through the dark –
       Brandy for the Parson,
        Baccy for the Clerk;
Them that asks no questions isn't told a lie –
Watch the wall, my darling, while the Gentlemen go by!

RUDYARD KIPLING

Recipe for a Hippopotamus Sandwich

A hippo sandwich is easy to make.
All you do is simply take
One slice of bread,
One slice of cake,
Some mayonnaise,
One onion ring,
One hippopotamus,
One piece of string,
A dash of pepper —
That ought to do it.
And now comes the problem . . .
Biting into it!

SHEL SILVERSTEIN

The Eagle

He clasps the crag with crooked hands;
Close to the sun in lonely lands,
Ring'd with the azure world, he stands.

The wrinkled sea beneath him crawls;
He watches from his mountain walls,
And like a thunderbolt he falls.

ALFRED, LORD TENNYSON

The Wild Dog

The City Dog goes to the drinking trough,
He waves his tail and laughs, and goes when he has had enough.
His intelligence is on the brink
Of human intelligence. He knows the Council will give him a drink.

The Wild Dog is not such an animal,
Untouched by human kind, he is inimical,
He keeps his tail stiff, his eyes blink,
And he goes to the river when he wants a drink.
He goes to the river, he stamps on the mud,
And at night he sleeps in the dark wood.

STEVIE SMITH

The Collier

When I was born on Amman hill
A dark bird crossed the sun.
Sharp on the floor the shadow fell,
I was the youngest son.

And when I went to the County School
I worked in a shaft of light.
In the wood of the desk I cut my name:
Dai for Dynamite.

The tall black hills my brothers stood;
Their lessons all were done.
From the door of the school when I ran out
They frowned to watch me run.

The slow grey bells they rung a chime
Surly with grief or age.
Clever or clumsy, lad or lout,
All would look for a wage.

I learned the valley flowers' names
And the rough bark knew my knees.
I brought home trout from the river
And spotted eggs from the trees.

A coloured coat I was given to wear
Where the lights of the rough land shone.
Still jealous of my favour
The tall black hills looked on.

They dipped my coat in the blood of a kid
And they cast me down a pit,
And although I crossed with strangers
There was no way up from it.

Soon as I went from the County School
I worked in a shaft. Said Jim,
'You will get your chain of gold, my lad,
But not for a likely time.'

And one said, 'Jack was not raised up
When the wind blew out the light
Though he interpreted their dreams
And guessed their fears by night.'

And Tom, he shivered his leper's lamp
For the stain that round him grew;
And I heard mouths pray in the after-damp
When the picks would not break through.

They changed words there in the darkness
And still through my head they run,
And white on my limbs is the linen sheet
And gold on my neck the sun.

VERNON WATKINS

Overheard On a Saltmarsh

Nymph, nymph, what are your beads?

Green glass, goblin. Why do you stare at them?

Give them me.

         No.

Give them me. Give them me.

              No.

Then I will howl all night in the reeds,
Lie in the mud and howl for them.

Goblin, why do you love them so?
They are better than stars or water,
Better than voices of winds that sing,
Better than any man's fair daughter,
Your green glass beads on a silver ring.

Hush I stole them out of the moon.

Give me your beads, I want them.

                                No.

I will howl in a deep lagoon
For your green glass beads, I love them so.
Give them me. Give them me.

                                No.

HAROLD MONRO

The Fallow Deer at the Lonely House

One without looks in to-night
    Through the curtain-chink
From the sheet of glistening white;
One without looks in to-night
    As we sit and think
    By the fender-brink.

We do not discern those eyes
    Watching in the snow;
Lit by lamps of rosy dyes
We do not discern those eyes
    Wondering, aglow,
    Fourfooted, tiptoe.

THOMAS HARDY

Mushrooms

Overnight, very
Whitely, discreetly,
Very quietly

Our toes, our noses
Take hold on the loam,
Acquire the air.

Nobody sees us,
Stops us, betrays us;
The small grains make room.

Soft fists insist on
Heaving the needles,
The leafy bedding,

Even the paving.
Our hammers, our rams,
Earless and eyeless,

Perfectly voiceless,
Widen the crannies,
Shoulder through holes. We

, silently, now the moon
s the night in her silver shoon;
way, and that, she peers, and sees
r fruit upon silver trees;
e by one the casements catch
r beams beneath the silvery thatch;
ouched in his kennel, like a log,
Vith paws of silver sleeps the dog;
om their shadowy cote the white breasts peep
f doves in a silver-feathered sleep;
harvest mouse goes scampering by,
ith silver claws, and silver eye;
nd moveless fish in the water gleam,
silver reeds in a silver stream.

LTER DE LA MARE

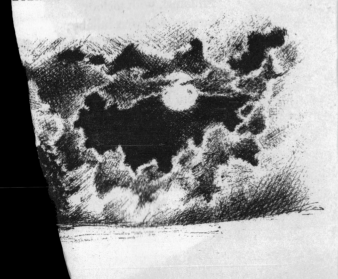

Diet on water,
On crumbs of shadow,
Bland-mannered, asking

Little or nothing.
So many of us!
So many of us!

We are shelves, we are
Tables, we are meek,
We are edible,

Nudgers and shovers
In spite of ourselves.
Our kind multiplies:

We shall by morning
Inherit the earth.
Our foot's in the door.

SYLVIA PLATH

Praise of a Collie

She was a small dog, neat and fluid —
Even her conversation was tiny:
She greeted you with *bow* never *bow-wow*.

Her sons stood monumentally over her
But did what she told them. Each grew grizzled
Till it seemed he was his own mother's grandfather.

Once, gathering sheep on a showery day,
I remarked how dry she was. Pollóchan said, 'Ah,
It would take a very accurate drop to hit Lassie.'

And her tact — and tactics! When the sheep bolted
In an unforeseen direction, over the skyline
Came — who but Lassie, and not even panting.

She sailed in the dinghy like a proper sea-dog.
Where's a burn? — she's first on the other side.
She flowed through fences like a piece of black wind.

But suddenly she was old and sick and crippled . . .
I grieved for Pollóchan when he took her a stroll
And put his gun to the back of her head.

NORMAN MacCAIG

You S

You spotte
    Thorny he
Newts and blin
    Come not near
        Philomel, with m
        Sing in our sweet lull
    Lulla, lulla, lullaby; lulla, lu
        Never harm,
        Nor spell nor charm,
    Come our lovely lady nigh;
    So, good night, with lullaby.

Weaving spiders, come not here;
    Hence, you long-legg'd spinners,
Beetles black, approach not near;
    Worm nor snail, do no offen
        Philomel, with melody,
        Sing in our sweet lull
    Lulla, lulla, lullaby;
        Never harm.
        Nor spell nor
    Come our love
    So, good nigl

WILLIAM SH

106

108

Copyright acknowledgments

The Hogarth Press for 'Beachcomber' and 'A Child's Calendar' from *Fishermen with Ploughs* by George Mackay Brown. Reprinted by permission of The Hogarth Press.

Felix Gluck Press for 'Wanted—A Witch's Cat' from *What Witches Do* by Sheila McGee. Reprinted by permission of Felix Gluck Press.

A. D. Peters and Co Ltd for 'a cat, a horse and the sun' by Roger McGough from *After the Merrymaking* published by Jonathan Cape Ltd. Reprinted by permission of A. D. Peters and Co Ltd.

Sebastian Mays for 'Moon Bat' by Sebastian Mays. Reprinted by permission of Sebastian Mays.

Ewart Milne for 'Diamond Cut Diamond' by Ewart Milne, originally published by The Bodley Head and also included in *The Faber Book of Children's Verse* edited by Janet Adam Smith. Reprinted by permission of Ewart Milne.

Cynthia Mitchell for 'A Skip to Beat Bad Temper' from *Halloweena Hecate and Other Rhymes to Skip To*, published by William Heinemann Ltd.

Atheneum Publishers Inc for Lilian Moore, 'Dragon Smoke' and 'Until I saw the sea' in *I Feel the Same Way*. Copyright © 1967 by Lilian Moore. Reprinted with the permission of Atheneum Publishers Inc.

Peter Mortimer for 'Bigtrousers Dan' and 'Babies are Boring' by Peter Mortimer. Reprinted by permission of Peter Mortimer.

Penguin Books Ltd for 'Winter Days', 'Real Life' and 'Cycling Down the Street to Meet my Friend John' from Gareth Owen, *Salford Road* (Kestrel Books 1979) pp 65, 50, 13; copyright © 1971, 1974, 1976, 1979 by Gareth Owen. Reprinted by permission of Penguin Books Ltd.

George Allen and Unwin for 'A Small Dragon' by Brian Patten from *Notes to the Hurrying Man* published by George Allen and Unwin. Reprinted by permission of George Allen and Unwin.

Ted Hughes for 'Mushrooms' from *The Colossus* by Sylvia Plath published by Faber and Faber Ltd, copyright © Ted Hughes 1967. Reprinted by permission of Ted Hughes.

Faber and Faber Ltd for 'In a Station of the Metro' by Ezra Pound. Reprinted by permission of Faber and Faber Ltd from *Collected Shorter Poems* by Ezra Pound.

Greenwillow Books for 'The Lion' from *Zoo Doings* by Jack Prelutsky. Copyright © 1974, 1983 by Jack Prelutsky. By permission of Greenwillow Books (A Division of William Morrow and Company).

Oxford University Press for 'Fireworks' by James Reeves. Reprinted by permission of Oxford University Press.

Vernon Scannell for 'Junk' and 'Intelligence Test' by Vernon Scannell. Reprinted by permission of Vernon Scannell.

Penguin Books Ltd for 'Disturbed, The Cat' by Karai Senryū from *The Penguin Book of Japanese Verse*, translated by Geoffrey Bownas and Anthony Thwaite (The Penguin Poets, 1964), p137. Copyright © 1964 Geoffrey Bownas and Anthony Thwaite. Reprinted by permission of Penguin Books Ltd.

Diet on water,
On crumbs of shadow,
Bland-mannered, asking

Little or nothing.
So many of us!
So many of us!

We are shelves, we are
Tables, we are meek,
We are edible,

Nudgers and shovers
In spite of ourselves.
Our kind multiplies:

We shall by morning
Inherit the earth.
Our foot's in the door.

SYLVIA PLATH

Praise of a Collie

She was a small dog, neat and fluid —
Even her conversation was tiny:
She greeted you with *bow* never *bow-wow*.

Her sons stood monumentally over her
But did what she told them. Each grew grizzled
Till it seemed he was his own mother's grandfather.

Once, gathering sheep on a showery day,
I remarked how dry she was. Pollóchan said, 'Ah,
It would take a very accurate drop to hit Lassie.'

And her tact — and tactics! When the sheep bolted
In an unforeseen direction, over the skyline
Came — who but Lassie, and not even panting.

She sailed in the dinghy like a proper sea-dog.
Where's a burn? – she's first on the other side.
She flowed through fences like a piece of black wind.

But suddenly she was old and sick and crippled . . .
I grieved for Pollóchan when he took her a stroll
And put his gun to the back of her head.

NORMAN MaCCAIG

You Spotted Snakes

You spotted snakes with double tongue,
  Thorny hedgehogs, be not seen;
Newts and blind-worms, do no wrong;
  Come not near our fairy queen.
    Philomel, with melody,
    Sing in our sweet lullaby;
  Lulla, lulla, lullaby; lulla, lulla, lullaby!
    Never harm,
    Nor spell nor charm,
  Come our lovely lady nigh;
  So, good night, with lullaby.

Weaving spiders, come not here;
  Hence, you long-legg'd spinners, hence!
Beetles black, approach not near;
  Worm nor snail, do no offence.
    Philomel, with melody,
    Sing in our sweet lullaby;
  Lulla, lulla, lullaby; lulla, lulla, lullaby!
    Never harm.
    Nor spell nor charm,
  Come our lovely lady nigh;
  So, good night, with lullaby!

WILLIAM SHAKESPEARE

Silver

Slowly, silently, now the moon
Walks the night in her silver shoon;
This way, and that, she peers, and sees
Silver fruit upon silver trees;
One by one the casements catch
Her beams beneath the silvery thatch;
Couched in his kennel, like a log,
With paws of silver sleeps the dog;
From their shadowy cote the white breasts peep
Of doves in a silver-feathered sleep;
A harvest mouse goes scampering by,
With silver claws, and silver eye;
And moveless fish in the water gleam,
By silver reeds in a silver stream.

WALTER DE LA MARE

Copyright acknowledgments

J. M. Dent and Sons for 'Encounter' from *Poems* 1935–1948 by Clifford Dyment. Reprinted by permission of J. M. Dent and Sons.

David Higham Associates Ltd for 'The Night Will Never Stay' by Eleanor Farjeon from *Silver Sand and Snow* published by Michael Joseph. Reprinted by permission of David Higham Associates Ltd.

McGraw-Hill Book Company for 'The Sandpiper' by Robert Frost from *The Little Whistler*. Reprinted by permission of McGraw-Hill Book Company.

The Estate of Robert Frost and Jonathan Cape Ltd for 'Stopping by Woods on a Snowy Evening' from *The Poetry of Robert Frost*, edited by Edward Connery Lathem. Reprinted by permission of The Estate of Robert Frost and Jonathan Cape Ltd.

Oxford University Press for 'A Peculiar Christmas' copyright © Roy Fuller 1983. From *Upright Downfall* (Three Poets Series, 1983). Reprinted by permission of Oxford University Press.

André Deutsch Ltd for 'In the Bathroom' from *Poor Roy* (André Deutsch 1977) by Roy Fuller. Reprinted by permission of André Deutsch Ltd.

The Society of Authors as the Literary Representative of the Estate of Rose Fyleman for 'Mice' by Rose Fyleman. Reprinted by permission of The Society of Authors as the Literary Representative of the Estate of Rose Fyleman.

Oxford University Press for 'The Late Express' copyright © Barbara Giles 1983. From *Upright Downfall* (Three Poets Series, 1983). Reprinted by permission of Oxford University Press.

David Higham Associates Ltd for 'The Starling' by John Heath-Stubbs from *The Bluefly in his Head* published by Oxford University Press. Reprinted by permission of David Higham Associates Ltd.

World's Work Ltd for 'Small, Smaller' by Russell Hoban from *The Pedalling Man*. Text copyright © 1968 by Russell Hoban. First published in Great Britain in 1969 by World's Work. Reprinted by permission of World's Work Ltd.

The National Trust and Macmillan London, Ltd for 'Smuggler's Song' and for 'The Way Through the Woods' from *Marlake Witches (Rewards and Fairies)* by Rudyard Kipling. Reprinted by permission of The National Trust and Macmillan London, Ltd.

Harlin Quist Ltd for 'Polar Bear' by Gail Kredenser. Reprinted by permission of Harlin Quist Ltd.

Faber and Faber Ltd for 'The Explosion' by Philip Larkin. Reprinted by permission of Faber and Faber Ltd from *High Windows* by Philip Larkin.

Macmillan of Canada, Ltd for 'The Muddy Puddle' from *Garbage Delight* by Dennis Lee. Reprinted by permission of Macmillan of Canada, Ltd.

George Macbeth for 'Old English Sheepdog' from *The Night-Stones* published by Macmillan London, Ltd and for 'Fourteen Ways of Touching the Peter' from *A Flock of Words* published by The Bodley Head. Reprinted by permission of George Macbeth.

The Hogarth Press for 'Aunt Julia' from *Selected Poems* and 'Praise of a Collie' from *Tree of Strings* by Norman MacCaig. Reprinted by permission of The Hogarth Press.

Index of authors and first lines

a cat mistrusts the sun, 75

A hippo sandwich is easy to make, 98

Ahlberg, Allan, 76

All winter through I bow my head, 64

An angry tiger in a cage, 43

And then I pressed the shell, 16

Anon, 31, 37, 51, 86, 92

At the edge of tide, 79

At the top of the house the apples are laid in rows, 44

Auden, W. H., 61

Aunt Julia spoke Gaelic, 18

Babies are boring, 82

Betjeman, John, 12

Biting air, 65

Bradman, Tony, 48

Breathe and blow, 72

Brownjohn, Alan, 58

Bunyan, John, 47

Causley, Charles, 49, 80

Clarke Moore, Clement, 90

Clark, Leonard, 77

Cole, William, 40

Colum, Padraic, 74

Come play with me, 81

Davies, William Henry, 73

de la Mare, Walter, 64, 84, 108

Disturbed, the cat, 21
Drinkwater, John, 44
Dyment, Clifford, 50
Eyes, 68
Farjeon, Eleanor, 51
Frost, Robert, 45, 79
Fuller, Roy, 41, 95
Fyleman, Rose, 31
Giles, Barbara, 23
Girls scream, 73
Hardy, Thomas, 103
Heath-Stubbs, John, 22
He clasps the crag with crooked hands, 98
Hoban, Russell, 15
Hood, Thomas, 70
I am sitting, 78
I'd sooner be, 56
I eat my peas with honey, 92
If you do not shake the bottle, 51
If you wake at midnight and hear a horse's feet, 96
I know that I shall meet my fate, 20
I'm glad that I, 21
In the land of Rumplydoodle, 88
I remember, I remember, 70
'Is anybody there?' said the Traveller, 84
I think mice, 31
I thought I'd win the spelling bee, 40
I thought that I knew all there was to know, 15
It's awf'lly bad luck on Diana, 12
It was a leisure day called 'holiday', 24

I've always wanted to live in a house, 48
I've found a small dragon in the woodshed, 36
I went into the wood one day, 37
I went out to the hazel wood, 11
Kipling, Rudyard, 62, 96
Kredenser, Gail, 92
Larkin, Philip, 28
Lee, Dennis, 78
Longfellow, Henry Wadsworth, 93
MacBeth, George, 26, 68
MacCaig, Norman, 18, 106
Mackay Brown, George, 32, 46
McGee, Shelagh, 39
McGough, Roger, 75
Mays, Sebastian, 67
Milne, Ewart, 66
Mitchell, Cynthia, 43
Monday, I found a boot, 32
Moore, Lilian, 29, 72
Mortimer, Peter, 82, 88
Munro, Harold, 52, 102
My Gramp has got a medal, 54
My Mum, 34
My parents kept me from the children who were rough, 69
No visitors in January, 46
Nymph, nymph, what are your beads?, 102
Once I held a bat, its small helpless, 67
One without looks in tonight, 103
On my bike and down our street, 38
On the day of the explosion, 28

O, to have a little house, 74
Out at the edge of town, 14
Overnight, very, 104
Over the grass a hedgehog came, 50
Owen, Gareth, 30, 38, 65
Patten, Brian, 36
Plath, Sylvia, 104
Poor prisoner in a cage, 77
Pound, Ezra, 29
Prelutsky, Jack, 53
Reeves, James, 33
Scannell, Vernon, 24, 55
Senryū, Karai, 21
Shakespeare, William, 107
She goes but softly, but she goeth sure, 47
She was a small dog, neat and fluid, 106
Silverstein, Shel, 98
Slowly, silently, now the moon, 108
Smith, Stevie, 37, 99
Snow? Absolutely not, 41
Spender, Stephen, 69
Spring is showery, flowery, bowery, 31
Squire, J. C., 94
Stephens, James, 16
Stevenson, Robert Louis, 42
Stop all the clocks, cut off the telephone, 61
Stuart, Derek, 54
Tennyson, Alfred, Lord, 98
The apparition of these faces in the crowd, 29
The City Dog goes to the drinking trough, 99

The codfish lays a million eggs, 37
The lion has a golden mane, 53
The night will never stay, 51
The ptarmigan is strange, 86
There's a train that runs through Hawthorn, 23
There was an Indian, who had known no change, 94
The secret of the polar bear, 92
The starling is my darling, although, 22
The summer nest uncovered by autumn wind, 87
The tide rises, the tide falls, 93
They rise like sudden fiery flowers, 33
They shut the road through the woods, 62
Thomas, Edward, 87
Thurman, Judith, 71, 95
Timothy Winters comes to school, 80
Tippett, James S., 21
'Twas the night before Christmas, when all through
the house, 90
Two cats, 66
Until I saw the sea, 29
Wanted—a witch's cat, 39
Watkins, Vernon, 100
We are going to see the rabbit, 58
What has happened to Lulu, mother?, 49
'What do you use your eyes for?', 55
What is that blood-stained thing, 95
Whenever the moon and stars are set, 42
When I go upstairs to bed, 76
When I was born on Amman hill, 100
When the mare shows you, 71

When the tea is brought at five o'clock, 52
white sun, 75
Whose woods these are I think I know, 45
Wright, Kit, 14, 34, 56
Yeats, W. B., 11, 20, 81
You can push, 26
'Yes,' thought John, 30
You spotted snakes with double tongue, 107

Blackbird Has Spoken

A brand new selection of Eleanor Farjeon's poetry which will delight readers of all ages.

Chosen by Anne Harvey

A Morning Song
For the First Day of Spring

*Morning has broken
Like the first morning,
Blackbird has spoken
Like the first bird.
Praise for the singing!
Praise for the morning!
Praise for them, springing
From the first Word.*

*Sweet the rain's new fall
Sunlit from heaven,
Like the first dewfall
In the first hour.
Praise for the sweetness
Of the wet garden,
Sprung in completeness
From the first shower.*

*Mine is the sunlight!
Mine is the morning
Born of the one light
Eden saw play.
Praise with elation,
Praise every morning
Spring's re-creation
Of the First Day!*

Peter Dixon's Grand Prix of Poetry

A chicane of flying verse by the Formula One poet, Peter Dixon, illustrated by David Thomas

Magic Cat

My mum whilst walking through the door spilt some
*   magic on the floor.*
Blobs of this
and splots of that
but most of it upon the cat.

Our cat turned magic, straight away
and in the garden went to play
where it grew two massive wings
and flew around in fancy rings.
'Oh look!' cried Mother, pointing high, 'I didn't know
our cat could fly.'
Then with a dash of Tibby's tail
she turned my mum into a snail!

So now she lives beneath a stone
and dusts around a different home.
And I'm an ant
and Dad's a mouse
and Tibby's living in our house.

Five Finger-Piglets

A veritable assortment of poetry by Carol Ann Duffy, Jackie Kay, Roger McGough, Gareth Owen and Brian Patten. Illustrated by Peter Bailey

Moon

'The moon is thousands of miles away,' My Uncle
    Trevor said.
Why can't he see
It's caught in a tree
Above our onion bed?

Gareth Owen

I'm Telling On You!

Poems about brothers and sisters, chosen by Brian Moses
and illustrated by Lucy Maddison

My baby brother's secrets

When my baby brother
wants to tell me a secret,
he comes right up close.
But instead of putting his lips
against my ear,
he presses his ear
tightly against my ear.
Then, he whispers so softly
that I can't hear
a word he is saying.

My baby brother's secrets
are safe with me.

John Foster

Teachers' Pets

Read all about Miss King's Kong, Mrs Cox's fox, Mr Spratt's tabby cat, Miss Cahoot's newts and many other extraordinary and talented teachers' pets!

Chosen by Paul Cookson and illustrated by David Parkins.

Classroom Helper

Can we borrow your chipmunk Miss?
He's such a useful pet,
So tidy and efficient,
Out best pencil sharpener yet!

Sue Cowling

Elephant Dreams

Poems by Ian McMillan, Paul Cookson and David Harmer,
illustrated by Lucy Maddison. All the very best from three
performing poets sandwiched together in one tasty volume.

Can't be Bothered to Think of a Title

*When they make slouching in the chair an Olympic
  sport
I'll be there.*

*When they give out a cup
for refusing to get up
I'll win it every year.*

*When they hand out the gold
for sitting by the fire
I'll leave the others in the cold,*

*and when I'm asked to sign my name
in the Apathetic Hall of Fame
I won't go.*

Ian McMillan

School Trips

Poems chosen by Brian Moses and illustrated by Lucy
Maddison.

Mysteries of the Universe

*We went by coach
to the planetarium
and saw the mysteries
of the Universe.*

*We saw the birth of stars,
black holes,
comets trailing cosmic dust,
and talked about
the existence of aliens.*

But a greater mystery awaited us all.

*When we left school
sixty-two of us boarded the coach.*

*When we arrived back at school
sixty-three of us got off.*

Roger Stevens

A selected list of poetry books
available from Macmillan

The Secret Lives of Teachers   0 330 34265 7
    Revealing rhymes, chosen by Brian Moses   £3.50

'Ere We Go!   0 330 32986 3
    Football poems, chosen by David Orme   £2.99

Aliens Stole My Underpants   0 330 34995 3
    Intergalactic poems chosen by Brian Moses   £2.99

Revenge of the Man-Eating Gerbils   0 330 35487 6
    And other vile verses, chosen by David Orme   £2.99

Teachers' Pets   0 330 36868 0
    Chosen by Paul Cookson   £2.99

Parent-Free Zone   0 330 34554 0
    Poems about parents, chosen by Brian Moses   £2.99

I'm Telling On You   0 330 36867 2
    Poems chosen by Brian Moses   £2.99